# VANCOUVERITES

## GEORGE ONSTOT

THIS BOOK IS DEDICATED TO
VANCOUVERITES
EVERYWHERE

# 1

This story is about a couple of Canadian men, two skinny, mostly unhappy older white guys who lived on a planet that was choking on its own vomit and feces.

One of them was a fiction writer named Willard Salmon, who was unknown at the time and believed that his best days, which had been less than good, were long gone. He was wrong; because of his meeting with the other man, Willard became famous.

Willard met Centrick Cline, who owned a Ford truck dealership. Centrick was having severe mental problems because his brain chemistry was out of whack most of the time.

Here's the deal: Both men were citizens and residents of Canada, an oversized, underpopulated country. Most of its citizens didn't know its national anthem, which was called O Canada, and many did not know that its capital was Ottawa, which was close to Montreal. Montreal was in Quebec, a mostly French-speaking place where sometimes they pretended not to speak English, just to annoy the people in English-speaking Canada. In America, the country is chopped up into pieces called "states." Most Canadians call America "the States"; in Canada, the country is chopped up into things called "provinces." Willard and Centrick lived in a province called British Columbia, named for Britain and Columbus, the guy credited with being the first white guy to set foot on North America.

The thing about Canada was that it had fewer people in it than the American state of California did. Canada was huge, with very few people and a very wimpy military. That was O.K.; Canadians woke up, went to work, got laid and went to sleep without worrying that a bigger, tougher country would invade them. There was this thing called the North Atlantic Treaty Organization (that everyone called N.A.T.O. for short), a military agreement signed by Canada, the States and some other countries. The agreement said, "If anyone invades you, we'll defend you, and if anyone invades us, you'll help us fight back." Since the States had the biggest and meanest military in the history of humankind, Canada knew it could lead a normal, happy life without having about a foreign invasion—sort of. Canada and the States had this things called the North American Free Trade Agreement—N.A.F.T.A—and became the biggest trade partners in human history. Canadians loved going down to the States to play and have fun, mainly because Canada was such a boring place.

?

In Canadian schools, teachers taught students about a certain year—1492—and made it sound as if 1492 was the year in which human beings discovered the New World. The teachers forgot that when Columbus and his boys hit land in Massachusetts—they thought they were in India—millions of people had already been living there for zillions of years. The year 1492 was simply the time that the Europeans arrived to take over the New World. Of course, the Europeans, when they first sailed to Massachusetts and met the red-skinned people who they thought were Indians, did not say, "Hi! We are here to steal your land and lives away." No, they came with smiles and handshakes and gave the red-skinned people blankets that were full of smallpox germs and smallpox killed off vast numbers of those people.

For generations, children here have asked, "How come we still call the Native North Americans 'Indians' even though they have nothing to do with India?" Teachers and parents say, "Ask me something else."

The European men, when they arrived in what is now called Massachusetts, had every intention of "invading" this huge piece of land and renaming it the United States of America, and that is what they did. They killed off the Natives with their diseases for which the Natives had built up no immunities, and they exploited and manipulated those Natives in every way they could think of.

?

When Centrick Cline and Willard Salmon first met, their country was the northern neighbor of the country that was by far the richest and most powerful country in human history. That country, the States, had more food, minerals and machinery than the others, and it had a reputation as the meanest and toughest country on the planet, so nobody would try to invade that country or Canada.

?

Centrick Cline and Willard Salmon lived in Canada, where there was still plenty of everything and no chance that a foreign invader would try to snatch it all away. Both Canada and the States believed that people who had lots of goodies should refuse to share their goodies with people who were broke and starving unless those rich people *wanted* to share their goodies, but most of them wanted to keep their goodies for themselves, so they did.

?

Each person in Canada and the States was supposed to keep as many goodies as he could. Some of those people grabbed lots of goodies, hoarded them, then grabbed more goodies and so on. Other people couldn't grab any goodies at all.

Centrick Cline was loaded down with goodies when he met Willard Salmon. As Centrick walked by, people whispered, "He's really loaded."

Here is how much Willard Salmon owned back then: -0-.

So Centrick Cline and Willard Salmon met in Vancouver during a literary arts festival in the year 2002.

Again, Centrick Cline was a Ford truck dealer who was mentally ill.

His mental illness was due mostly to a shortage (or excess) of neurohormones like serotonin, dopamine and others, but that same mental illness made him take seriously weird and bad ideas instead of laughing them off the way mentally healthy people would.

The bad and weird ideas that hurt Centrick Cline came to him from Willard Salmon, who supposed himself so harmless that he might actually be dead.

Sometimes he said aloud, "We would all be better

off if I was dead."

But then he met Centrick Cline and discovered that he was alive enough to make another human being profoundly mentally disturbed.

Here was the main idea that Willard Salmon gave to Centrick Cline that unhinged Centrick so much: He told Centrick that all people on Earth were brainless machines except for one—Centrick Cline.

Of all the billions of people on Earth, only Centrick had the capacity to think, feel, dream and hurt. Everyone else was just an android, a machine that did its thing and went its way until it keeled over and died. Centrick was an experiment that God, or whatever you wanted to call the Supreme Being, was involved in.

No one took Willard Salmon seriously. He saved up his bad and weird ideas and put them into a science-fiction novel, which was where Centrick found them. The novel was not intended to be read only by Centrick; Willard hadn't yet met him while writing the book. Instead, Centrick wrote it for anyone and everyone who cared it read it. His message to the reader was, "You're the only one alive who is a thinking, feeling person. Aren't you the lucky one?"

It just about destroyed Centrick Cline.

# 2

Centrick Cline, a widower, lived in Point Grey, the most exclusive residential area in Vancouver. Every house there cost millions of dollars.

Centrick's only companion was a black Labrador named Ringo. Ringo had been in dozens of brutal fights with other dogs over the years and lost as many fights as he won.

Centrick had an Indian housekeeper named Appendy Patel who kept his home tidy. She also cooked and served him his dinner. Then she took the bus home to a suburb called Surrey. Appendy had lived in Canada for twenty years. She had emigrated from Bhopal, India.

Appendy and Centrick spoke little to each other even though they liked one another just fine. Centrick saved us most of his conversation for his dog. He and Ringo would play-wrestle on the floor. Centrick would say, "How's my big boy, eh? How's my big boy?"

Appendy considered her boss strange but nice, so when Centrick started to become mentally ill, she really didn't pay much attention.

?

Willard Salmon was alone, too, but his companion was a parrot, Kit. While Centrick sweet-talked his dog, Willard spoke to his bird about the inevitable earthquake.

"It'll kill us all, Kit. We'll deserve it, too. We have it coming."

He told his pet that of all humankind's sins, the worst was our abuse of the planet. "We're all barbarians, Kit. We think we can pollute our planet and that it will purify itself. Maybe we'll have to move to Mars because Earth will have become incapable of supporting life."

?

Another thing Salmon did that people might have considered weird was he called mirrors *thieves*. He laughed when he thought that mirrors were things that stole away a bit of your essence each time you looked at them.

He would amuse himself by admonishing a child, "Stay away from that thief. It'll steal you away."

By the time he died, everyone called mirrors thieves. That was how much of a cultural impact he'd had.

?

In 2002, Salmon lived in a puny apartment in Montreal, Quebec. He worked as an installer of aluminum siding. He did not work as a member of the sales force—because he lacked *charisma*. Charisma was the ability of making people like you even though they didn't know you and you didn't know them.

?

Centrick Cline had lots of charisma.

?

I have lots of charisma, too, or so I'm told.

?

Many people have lots of charisma, or so they're told.

?

Salmon's boss and colleagues did not know that he was a writer. No publishing company worth being published by had ever heard of him even though he had written one hundred thirty-one novels and over two thousand short stories by the time he met Centrick Cline.

Scarcely aware of the existence of computers, he wrote all of his fiction on a manual typewriter and made no copies. He mailed his manuscripts without enclosing self-addressed, stamped envelopes; sometimes he didn't even bother to notify the publisher of his mailing address. He found the names and addresses of publishing houses large and small from the writer's magazines he read for free in public libraries. That was how he got to know about Global Classics Library, a company that published hardcore pornography in West Hollywood, California. They ran his stories, which seldom included female characters and never had sexual content, so that a one-hundred-page nudie book would become a two-hundred-page nudie book.

The publisher told him nothing about where or when they would use his stories. They always paid him $0.00.

?

Since they had no idea of how to contact him, they did not send him author's copies of the stories he sent them and they published. Sometimes he found his published stories by seeking them out in pornography stores. They changed the names of his stories; "Outer Space Adventurers" became "Foreign Fuck Monsters."

He wrote a novel about a man on Earth named Silvo Gorsek. Silvo was a bachelor but lived in a society where everyone had a huge family. So Silvo, a scientist, figured out a way to clone himself using Top Ramen noodles. He would shave his armpit hair, mix with the shavings with the noodles and expose the mixture to cosmic rays. The result would always be a large number of humans who looked exactly like Silvo Gorsek. He got carried away and made hundreds of clones at a time. Everyone praised him because their culture had taught them that having lots of babies was a good thing even if you couldn't afford to feed them.

That's just how it was.

?

Gorsek discovered that he could not feed and clothe his huge family, so he urged his politicians to pass laws prohibiting gigantic families. They said that it was a free country where people should have huge families if that's what they wanted. But they did pass strict laws concerning the possession of Top Ramen.

That's just how it was.

The illustrations that disturbed Salmon were grainy photographs of a few white women taking turns sucking the cock of a smiling black man.

When he met Centrick Cline, Willard Salmon's best-known book was *Judgment Day*. The publisher left the title intact but obscured most of Willard Salmon's name with big lurid letters saying FOR MEN WHO THINK PINK! LOOK INSIDE!

To "think pink" referred to the color of a woman's vagina and a man's obsession with it. Men in a polite society were not supposed to look at or think about vaginas unless they were doctors. Therefore some enterprising men decided they could make money by taking pictures of vaginas and sell them to other men.

?

When Willard Salmon accepted the Nobel Prize for Medicine in 2005, he said, "I predict that in the years ahead human beings will be the only animals left on this planet. We'll all become vegans because there will be no meat left to eat unless we become cannibals, and I'm not altogether sure that's such a bad idea."

# 3

Willard Salmon received relatively few fan letters but one arrived from an eccentric millionaire who spent thousands of dollars on a private detective to get Salmon's address because Salmon had made himself so difficult to locate.

The letter arrived at his basement apartment. It was written in big cursive and Salon thought at first that its author might be about twelve years old. The letter said that Judgment Day was the best novel ever written and Willard Salmon, if he was American, should be president of the United States.

Salmon said to his dog, "Well, Ringo, things are improving. Check this out." He read the letter aloud. Nothing about it indicated that its author, Eugene Sweetlove, was a fabulously affluent man.

?

Willard Salmon had had a dreary and depressing

childhood despite living in Vancouver, which was considered a very desirable place to live in. The despondency that wracked him in later life, that ruined his three marriages, which caused his only child, Blondie, to run away from home as a teenager, very likely had to do with all the rain that fell in Vancouver, a really wet city.

?

Alas, the fan letter came too late. It contained bad news; Willard Salmon considered it a horrible invasion of privacy. In his letter, Sweetlove promised to make him famous. What Salmon said, heard only by his dog, was, "Mind your own bloody business."

?

I invented Willard Salmon. I'm glad I did, most of the time.

I gave him an overbite. I made his hair white and long. I also gave him legs that were ugly and thin, that cramped up at night when he tried to go to sleep.

After he received his first fan letter, I made him

receive an invitation to attend, and be a speaker at, the literary arts festival at the University of British Columbia.

?

That letter was from Barry Doyle, the festival's chairman. He respected, admired and adored Willard Salmon. He implored Salmon to be one of the distinguished Canadian participants at the five-day festival. It would celebrate the opening of the Kimberly Doyle Centre for the Literary Arts at the University of British Columbia.

Although the letter did not say so, Kimberly Doyle was the deceased mother of the festival's chairman, Barry Doyle, one of Vancouver's wealthiest residents. He had paid for the brand-new Centre for the Literary Arts, which everyone said looked like an upside-down sake cup.

Barry Doyle was exactly the same age as Willard Salmon, but the two men scarcely resembled each other. In fact, Barry Doyle did not even look Caucasian any longer. Desiring to keep a year-round tan, he got too many sessions on a tanning bed and ended up looking like a prosperous, grinning black man. Even black men thought he was a black man. Canada had very few black men, but they thought he was one of them.

?

In his letter, Barry Doyle said he had never actually read any of Willard Salmon's novels but would surely do so before they met at the festival. He said, "Eugene Sweetlove speaks very highly of you. He says you're the very finest Canadian novelist there is. What higher praise is there than that?"

Paperclipped to the letter was a check for five thousand dollars. "That is your fee, if you accept this engagement," said the letter.

Salmon whistled as he looked at the check. That was a great deal of money, more than he had had in a long while.

?

Here is the reason Salmon was invited to speak at that event: Barry Doyle very much wanted to have a masterpiece painting to put on a wall during the festival. Despite being wonderfully stinking rich, he could not afford to buy one, so he arranged to borrow one.

The first person he approached was Eugene Lovely, who owned a Rembrandt worth millions of dollars. Lovely agreed to lend the Rembrandt if Doyle would hire as a speaker the greatest English-language alive, who was named Willard Salmon.

Salmon laughed aloud and admitted that he loved being flattered, but then he started to worry. He always worried when he felt someone was messing in his personal business. He turned to his dog and said, "Why are these people so interested in Willard Salmon?"

He read the letter again. He said to his dog, "They want Salmon to wear a *tuxedo*, Ringo. This can't be for real."

Then he said, "Ringo, they want me because they know I already own a tuxedo." Salmon did, indeed, own one, and had packed it around for a few decades because it had cost so much money and he knew that at some point he would have some reason to put it on again.

"I'm not sure this is a good idea," he said to Ringo. "I could go there and try to deliver a speech but I would make such a fool of myself that I would become the laughingstock of the University of British Columbia. So I won't go. I'll cash the check and spend the money, but to hell with this tuxedo and the invitation."

?

Salmon ultimately accepted the invitation. He took some of the money and used it to travel to New York City so he could go into some pornographic bookstores and search for his novels. He did not have any copies of his own books at home. He loathed his own work and wanted to read some of it to the crowd at the festival so they, too, could know how awful it was.

# 4

Centrick just kept getting more and more mentally ill. He saw a smiling face on the moon; it kept blowing him kisses as he stood and gazed at it from just outside the Barry Doyle Centre for the Arts. The next day, he saw a green cop, twenty feet tall, directing traffic at the intersection of Willingdon and Gilmore. He said nothing about it to anyone. He kept it all to himself.

His mental illness got fed up with being Centrick's little secret. His disease decided it wasn't enough to think weird things; he needed to start *speaking* and *acting* in weird ways, too.

His illness said, "You need to be proud of me."

?

Later on, everyone shook his head and felt badly about failing to observe that Centrick was becoming mentally irregular. After he went berserk, the local media reported on him extensively and admonished everyone to pay attention to others' "peculiar" behavior and urge those acting-out people to seek professional help right away.

But Centrick wasn't all that odd before he met Willard Salmon. Agnes Semko, the Caucasian woman who was Centrick's secretary and sex partner, said that her man seemed perfectly happy right up until the time he wigged out.

"It seemed to me," she told a reporter, "that he appeared to be recovering from his wife's suicide."

?

Agnes worked for Centrick at a place called Centrick Cline's Ford Trucks on Kingsway Street, right next door to the new Best Western hotel.

Agnes believed that Centrick was feeling well and enjoying life because he had started singing, loudly and without embarrassment; often he sang the songs he'd just heard on the radio. Centrick, who had never shown an interest in singing or even listening to music, now crooned as he sat at his desk or took customers on test drives. One afternoon, while crossing  the Best Western's lobby, he belted out a tune, smiling and pointing at passersby as if he were the star of an M-G-M musical. But nobody felt alarmed by his behavior, especially since most of his audience knew who he was and that he owned part of the property.

A Native bus boy and a Native waiter shook their heads and chuckled at each other.

"Check him out," said the bus boy. "Singin' like a bloody fool an' he don't care what anyone thinks."

"When you're as rich as he is," the waiter replied, "you don't *have* to care what other people think."

?

The only person who said anything about Centrick's mental illness was Harri Singh, the sales manager at Centrick Cline Ford Trucks. About a month before Centrick flipped out, Harri said to Agnes, "Something's wrong with Centrick. I think he needs a shrink."

Harri knew Centrick better than virtually everyone else did. He had known Centrick for two decades. Harri started working for Centrick back when much of Kingsway Street was scrubland.

"I've known Centrick for so long that it's hard for me to remember when I *didn't* know him. Back in the early days, there just wasn't that much traffic on Kingsway and we didn't know if the truck dealership would survive. The Centrick of today acts in weird ways that I don't remember from back then."

?

It was true that Centrick had taken a risk by opening such a huge truck dealership on Kingsway Street back then. White people were the only ones with enough money to buy new vehicles. Later on, Asian and Indian gangsters wanted BMWs and they usually paid cash.

?

The way Centrick got the money to start the Ford

truck dealership was by borrowing the money from Lower Mainland National Bank. For collateral, he put up his stock in a company called *Prairie Mining Incorporated.* He had lots of stock and it kept increasing in value because Canada was full of valuable stuff that needed to be dug out of the ground.

?

Harri Singh said to Agnes, "When you've been working with someone for a long enough time, you get a sense of how they are as a person. I've been working with Centrick long enough to know that something's going on with him right now. If you don't believe me, ask Vernal Braithwaite."

Vernal Braithwaite was a white mechanic who had been working for Centrick since day one. Vernal's wife was schizophrenic, and her bad days had been outnumbering her good ones. She was so erratic that Vernal was in no position to gauge Centrick's mood swings. Vernal's wife, Susan, had convinced herself that Vernal was trying to kill her, and each time he woke up in the middle of the night to use the washroom she woke up, too, and hid under their bed so he wouldn't have a chance to stab her to death.

?

"Harri," said Agnes, "Centrick is the most even-tempered person I know. He has fewer bad days than other people, so he's entitled to one every once in a while. Sometimes we forget that he's human like everyone else."

"But why should he pick on *me*?" Harri had a valid point: Centrick *had* singled him out for abuse that day.

In the days ahead, Centrick would hurt many others, including visitors from Saskatchewan, but Harri was his only victim for the time being.

?

"Why did this happen to *me*?" asked people in Vancouver. They asked that question as paramedics scraped them off the roadway and loaded them into ambulances. They asked that as they were being arrested for public drunkenness or punched in the nose. "Why did this happen to *me*?"

"I guess," said Agnes, "that he believed you were someone who could put up with some of his abuse on one of his bad days."

"How would *you* have liked it if he had criticized *your* clothing?" For that was what Centrick did that so offended Harri—he said nasty things about Harri's style of dress.

"Remind yourself," said Agnes, "that Centrick is the best boss around." She was right; Centrick paid the highest salaries in town. His dental plan was very generous. He paid out Christmas bonuses and had a profit-sharing plan. Working at Centrick Cline Ford Trucks could be very lucrative because those vehicles mostly sold themselves. Centrick's salespeople were often just order-takers. Their boss kept his door open in case any of his employees wished to speak to him about matters professional or personal.

On the day he criticized Harri Singh's clothing, Centrick Cline spent over an hour with Vernal Braithwaite on the subject of Harri's wife's mental illness. "She wigs out and talks crazy shit," he told Centrick.

"Maybe she just needs rest," said Centrick.

"Maybe I'm wigging out, too," said Vernal. "I go home and talk to my dog for hours."

"That's what he's there for."

?

Here is what happened between Centrick and Harri that made Harri so upset:

Harri entered Centrick's office just as soon as Vernal left. Harri expected a friendly conversation with Centrick because the two men, in all the years they had known each other, had never had a dispute nor conflict of any significance.

"How's it goin', eh?" Harri asked Centrick.

"What's on your mind? Got a problem?"

"No problem here."

"Vernal's wife thinks he's trying to kill her."

"Too bad." Then, just to keep up his end of the conversation, Harri said, "Sometimes I regret the fact that I didn't have children. But then I remind myself of how overpopulated the world is and how cruel so many people are."

Centrick shrugged.

"Maybe," Harri continued, "we should have adopted a kid, just so we would sort of feel like a family. But it's too late for that now. As it is, my old lady and I have fun spending all of our money on ourselves."

Centrick looked up, his eyes blazing with fury. "Harri, why don't you donate your whole wardrobe to the Sally Ann? I always feel like I'm looking at an Indian Donald Trump." Donald Trump, the brash businessman who had just been elected president of the States, was a man who *always* wore blue suits, white shirts and solid-colored ties.

Harri just stood there for a few moments, then frowned. In all the years he and Centrick had known each other, the boss had never said an unkind word about the sales manager's attire. Yes, Harri *did* dress exactly like Donald Trump, but Harri wanted to come across as businesslike and professional.

"Look, Harri," Centrick said with a scowl, "Aloha time is coming up, and I need you to put all your clothes into Glad bags, dump them off at the Sally Ann and get some new threads. Otherwise, get yourself a new job at some men's store that sells lame stuff like the shit you're so fond of wearing."

?

Harri just stood there as if Centrick had just busted him in the nuts. The Aloha Week Centrick had mentioned was a promotion during which the indoor section of the dealership would be done up to look like Hawaii. People who bought new or used trucks, or ordered repairs costing in excess of one thousand dollars, were automatically entered into a draw for a free trip to Hawaii.

"Harri, I don't mind that you're a Paki with a big nose," Centrick said. "You can't really help those things. But there are things you *can* help. Friday will be a holiday. When you come back to work on Monday, I expect you to be a changed man, literally."

Friday was a holiday called Remembrance Day. On that day, people were supposed to think about the soldiers who had died defending Canada from foreign intruders.

"We make all of our money selling *trucks*, Harri," said Centrick. "People who buy *trucks* are mostly men and they like to think of themselves as rugged and tough. So why the fuck do you come here to work looking like Donald Trump? I'm sure Donald Trump has never driven a truck in his life."

Harri felt too heartbroken to point out that, even in his Donald Trump suits, he had the best sales record of anyone in the Lower Mainland. He understand trucks and knew that people in British Columbia bought them because they were rugged, practical vehichles. Nobody had ever questioned Harri Singh's professional competency. Until now.

?

Centrick Cline said, "Aloha Days will permit you to lighten up and loosen up, Harri. Show the world that you can have fun and smile.

"Harri! Have you noticed that there are colors in

the world that are not limited to blue, black, gray and white? Check out some of those vibrant colors and incorporate them into your wardrobe. Also, the Royal Canadian Mounted Police has just announced that they will *not* arrest people for smiling during work hours! Plus, the premier of British Columbia has personally told me that *nobody* will be charged with a sexual offense and be sent to Rainford Prison just for cracking a joke!"

?

Harri might not have felt so badly about Centrick's dressing-down, so to speak, if it weren't for the fact that he was a secret cross-dresser. On weekends he and his wife liked to close their drapes and she would help him get into his favorite ladies' underwear and dresses. At such times he felt truly alive and was being himself.

Only his wife knew about his cross-dressing sessions.

When Centrick ragged on him about his clothing and said something about Rainford Prison, Harri assumed that Centrick knew about the cross-dressing. Harri believed that British Columbia was an old-fashioned place and that cross-dressing was some sort of crime for which a person could be fined thousands of dollars and locked up for many years.

?

So Harri spent an awful Remembrance Day weekend fretting over things. But Centrick's weekend was worse.

Centrick's mental illness got the better of him to the point where he rushed to get out of bed at three or four in the morning, reach under his pillow, take out his Glock nine-millimeter automatic and stick it into his mouth. The handgun was a weapon made specifically for one person to shoot himself or another person.

In Canada, it was harder for people to get handguns than it was in the States. In Canada, the logic went that only the police and military people needed handguns, not the civilians. But civilians such as Centrick Cline had them, too. Centrick Cline believed that he needed one to protect himself and his goodies from those people who had no goodies and wanted him to share his with them whether he wanted to or not.

?

Sometimes, in the States, unhappy, mentally ill people would buy handguns and shoot famous people so that those mentally ill people could spend the rest of their lives bragging, "I shot this famous person." Back in 1980, a fat guy in Hawaii or somewhere else said, "I am going to New York City and shoot John Lennon."

Everyone who knew that fat guy believed he did not have enough intelligence to buy a gun, fly out to New York City and shoot that legendary musician. But the fat guy did exactly that; he even hung out near the front entrance of Lennon's building for much of the day waiting for the chance to shoot Lennon. Inside of the fat guy's jacket was a pocket, and inside of that pocket was a handgun. Nobody could see his handgun, so nobody knew he was going to shoot John Lennon with it. That was called "carrying a concealed weapon." If that fat guy had been carrying a rifle, he could not have concealed it in his pocket and would have had to hold it in his hands, in full view of everyone, and people would have said, "Why are you carrying that rifle? Are you going to shoot John Lennon or something?" If that fat guy had been carrying a deadly weapon in full view of others, he very likely would not have gotten the opportunity to shoot John Lennon. Afterwards, people said, "That fat guy who shot John Lennon looked very suspicious as he stood outside Lennon's building. Why didn't someone call the cops?"

Remaining in one public place for a prolonged time is called "loitering" and it freaks people out, so they call the cops.

?

Centrick decided against shooting himself. He put down the gun and reminded himself that even if he had pulled the trigger, nobody would have heard the shot; all of the houses in his neighborhood were far too well insulated for sounds to get in or out.

?

Centrick put on the floodlights and played basketball on his own private court.

His dog Ringo came out to spend some time with his best friend. Ringo lay down off to the side and gently wagged his tail as Centrick shot baskets.

"You and me, Ringo. Just the two of us," said Centrick. Sometimes he thought that Ringo was the only true friend he had in the entire world.

Nobody saw them because his entire house was shielded from view by tall trees and shrubs plus a tall cedar fence.

?

He put away the basketball and climbed into a Honda Accord he had taken in trade a few days earlier. Centrick sold Ford trucks and would sell the Accord to someone who carried used vehicles of all kinds, but first he would drive it around just for his own enjoyment.

He backed out of his driveway and rolled down the window. As his way of explaining to his neighbors why he, the Lower Mainland's most prominent Ford dealer, was driving a Honda, he shouted, "Just for my own enjoyment!" and honked his horn.

?

Centrick zoomed down South West Marine Drive and ended up on the TransCanada Highway. His was the only vehicle around. He swerved into an exit at a ridiculously high rate of speed, smashed into a guardrail, spun around numerous times and came out on Gilmore Avenue. He kept going backwards for some time, then ended up in a vacant lot. Presently he realized that he owned that lot.

He sat in silence for several minutes. Nobody heard the racket he'd made; nobody came by to see if anyone was hurt. A police officer was supposed to drive by every hour or so, but the nearest officer was curled up in his cruiser, sound asleep.

?

Centrick remained in his vacant lot for some time. He felt no need to leave, since it was his property and therefore he had every right to stay there as long as he pleased. He turned on the radio and listened to XM, the satellite service.

"I love rock 'n' roll," he said aloud. He *did* love it. He reminded himself to try to buy a rock-music radio station in Vancouver. He wanted to own more of everything. It seemed that whatever he bought, it became more available because *he* owned it. He guessed he was lucky that way.

# 5

While Centrick listened to Sirius satellite radio, Willard Salmon sat in a New York City movie theatre, his eyes closed, his brain trying to sleep. Times Square had been gentrified but a few all-night movie houses remained, and they were much cheaper than paying for a hotel room. Salmon had never done such a thing and supposed that doing so now was beneath him. For some weird reason, his goal was to arrive in Vancouver as the grubbiest of all old men. He had agreed to participate in a symposium out in Vancouver called "The Canadian Novel in the Twenty-first Century." He felt very tempted to go there and say something like, "I don't know anything about the Canadian novel in this century, but I *do* know something about spending the night in a funky old Manhattan picture show. Let's talk about *that* instead."

He also wanted to ask, "Did Marshall McLuhan

know anything about the relationship between pornographic images and book sales? Because many of my stories have been in books that are mostly women with their legs spread and pussies wide open."

?

Willard Salmon had spent much time that day in Manhattan stores that sold pornographic books. He had bought a couple of his own books, *Judgment Day* and *What the Man Doesn't Want You to Know*. He also bought a tuxedo shirt.

Salmon sat with his new purchases in his lap. He liked buying things; he didn't buy things often enough.

?

The dust jackets of the two books Willard Salmon bought contained promises of moist vaginas inside. The book containing the material that drove Centrick Cline insane was *What the Man Doesn't Want You to Know*, and its dust jacket showed a college professor being stripped nude by some naked coeds.

Naturally, there was nothing whatsoever in Salman's story about a naked professor and sorority girls. The story was about God and His messages to the only person on Earth who was totally free.

?

He bought a copy of a magazine called *Black Booty* because it contained one of his stories even though he had no idea that it had been accepted for publication. The date on the magazine indicated that it was over a decade old. He found it in a bin with a bunch of other boring magazines near the front of the store. The magazines were for people with panty fetishes.

When Salmon bought *Black Booty*, the cashier probably thought he was intoxicated or mentally retarded. The cashier knew that those magazines in the bin contained nothing but pictures of women wearing nothing but panties. The women had their legs spread and their vaginas open but they were wearing panties so you couldn't see their open vaginas. Those magazines were a rip-off compared to the more explicit magazines in the back of the store.

"Have fun," the cashier told Salmon. He meant that he hoped the pictures would give Salmon an erection so that he could masturbate till he ejaculated. That was the only reason people bought those books and magazines.

"It's for professional purposes," retorted Salmon.

# 6

Centrick Cline sat in the driver's seat of the used Mustang convertible, listening to the radio. As the owner of many businesses, he advertised heavily in radio, on TV and billboards and busboards, so he knew a few things about broadcasting. He knew, as he tuned into one station after another, that in downtown Vancouver, where most of that city's radio stations were located, practically all of those stations had broadcast booths that were empty all night. When he tuned into 1410 AM or 980 FM, the programming he heard came from Los Angeles or New York or somewhere—but not from Vancouver. The miracle of high technology had made "syndication" possible. Syndication meant that high technology made it possible for a guy in Los Angeles or New York to sit in a broadcast booth and have his show transmitted throughout Vancouver because the Vancouver radio bosses paid to have the show broadcast on their radio stations.

Centrick thought it was too bad. To him, people who were up at three in the morning should be able to hear what a Vancouver broadcaster had to say at that late hour.

?

While Centrick Cline sat there alone, at a nearby hospital, Vancouver's oldest resident lay dying and nobody cared very much. Fariel Subedar, one hundred five years old, had done the laundry for Centrick Cline's family for a few months back when Centrick was a small child. She told him about her years in India and how male agricultural workers were often bitten by kraits as they worked. They didn't feel the bites because the snakes' fangs were so sharp and tiny. But they knew they had been bitten because they woke up in the middle of the night unable to breathe and had seen many of their friends and relatives die that way.

?

An Indian doctor at the hospital watched Fariel Subedar die.

The doctor did not know her even though they had both come to Canada from the same country. His name was Jaz Johal and he had been in Vancouver only a short while. Jaz Johal felt he had little in common with Fariel Subedar or any of the other many Indians he met in Vancouver. The only other people in Vancouver he felt he could relate to were other doctors.

As she died, Fariel felt as alone in the world as Centrick Cline or Willard Salmon. Childlesss, she had no relatives and had made no effort to make friends with other Indians or other people in general, so when she lay on her deathbed she had no one but Jaz Singh to stand there and watch her die. She spoke her very last words to Jaz Singh, and she was too weak to say much.

Here is what she said just before she died: "Unnnhhhh."

?

Like all other people, Indians or otherwise, Fariel Subedar as she died sent invisible clouds of energy to all who had known her during her lifetime. She sent one such cloud to Centrick Cline, eleven miles away.

What he heard, somewhere in his mind, was this: "Unnnhhh."

?

Centrick Cline's mental illness now made him put his car in gear. He exited the vacant lot and cruised down Prairie Avenue.

He drove just past his main place of business, which was called Centrick Cline Ford Trucks, and he turned into the parking lot of the Best Western next door. He owned a third of the Best Western—in partnership with Vancouver's most popular orthodontist, Dr. Arthur Hayes, and Mel Billitz, who ran the parole board at Rainford Prison.

Centrick Cline went up the Best Western's back steps to the roof without encountering anyone. He looked up and saw a full moon. He thought for a moment of the Centre for the Literary Arts at the

University of British Columbia and wondered why they had designed it to look like an upside-down sake cup.

?

Centrick Cline looked out over the slumbering city. He had been born in Vancouver and spent his first three years in an orphanage about ten minutes away from the Best Western where he now stood. He had been adopted and educated in the city.

He now owned the Ford dealership, a piece of the Best Western, three Maple Leaf Burgers franchises, radio station CYVR, a half-dozen coin-operated car washes, three miniature golf courses and four downtown parking lots. His investment portfolio included positions in many lucrative companies.

But now he felt unsure of everything, even standing there in the city where he had spent his entire life. "*Who* am I? *Where* am I?" he called out in the middle of the night.

He reminded himself that his wife had drunk and drugged herself to death. He imagined that she hadn't suffered much—she'd just drunk down the vodka and swallowed the pills, collapsed, lost consciousness and died. He also reminded himself that his only child, Jay, had grown up to be a rubber-wristed, swishing homosexual. Everyone called him "Blondie." He played piano at the cocktail lounge of the new Best Western.

"Who am I? Where am I?" asked Centrick Cline.

# 7

Willard Salmon took a piss in the Manhattan porn theatre. He saw a handwritten message on the wall promising sexual favors to everyone who called a certain local telephone number.

"The universe is full of abundance," Salmon said aloud.

Also on the wall was a message that said, "What is the key to a happy life?"

Salmon checked hos pockets, came up with a felt pen and wrote his reply on the wall:

*To work and to love—*
*that is the key to a happy life,*
*you idiot.*

He went back into the auditorium and watched the movie some more. He thought of his own advice about happiness and decided that he had done more than his share of work already. But work and *love*? He wasn't sure he knew what love was, or how to do it. Once the movie ended, he saw the house lights come on. A middle-aged man who had sold him his ticket was now sweeping filthy debris from between the seats.

"Show's over, Gramps," said the man. "Go home now."

Salmon nodded but did not leave immediately. He observed a big metal box in the auditorium. It contained the movie and sound system and projector. A wire connected the box to the screen, and that was how the movie ended up on the screen. On the side of the box was a switch that said ON/OFF. He told himself that if he merely switched it back to ON, the intercourse and fellatio and ejaculations would resume. He marveled at the miracle of it all.

"I said goodnight," the man told him.

Salmon shrugged. "That machine. It fulfills such need. You just have to turn *it* on and it turns *you* on."

# 8

Willard Salmon left the porn theatre and walked around Times Square. The whole city was dangerous, partly because so many people carried handguns and because so many people were born with bad chemicals in their heads, then they bought more bad chemicals and added those to the ones already there.

?

The reason that people put those bad chemicals into their bodies was that, for fifteen minutes to an hour, those chemicals made those people feel better than they had ever felt before, because the bad chemicals make the brain release too much *dopamine*, a brain chemical that makes people feel good. The people who used crack and meth lived in ugly places and had no hope of moving into better places, so they used those bad chemicals as a way of escaping the ugliness for a while.

Salmon knew that new illegal chemicals were coming along all the time. He saw a white kid a few feet away lay sprawled on the sidewalk. The newest bad chemical was a sedative for elephants. Salmon wondered if that kid was under the influence of elephant sedatives.

?

Salmon felt terrified out there in Times Square. The Square had given him a life not worth living, yet I had given him an unshakable will to live. Many people had both qualities.

The theatre manager told everyone to leave because it was time to go home. He locked the doors and started to walk away.

A couple of young black prostitutes approached Salon and the manager and asked if they wanted some company. They were happy and friendly because they had just smoked crystal methamphetamine that made them feel much better than they should. The girls were country bumpkins from Mississippi whose ancestors had come to America to work as human machinery. The white farmers in America weren't using human machinery any longer; they had switched over to metal machinery because it would work endless hours without complaint and never asked for time off to eat and sleep.

So these black machines had to leave the American South because they weren't wanted anywhere else.

In the city, the black females now worked for pimps. Those men were the closest thing to God the females had ever met. Those pimps took away the women's free will, which the females didn't especially want anyway; having no free will meant that there was always someone to make their decisions for them. In church they had heard the preacher say, "Surrender yourself to Jesus," so what they did was, they met a tall black pimp who called himself Jesus and they surrendered themselves to him.

Their childhoods ended very soon. They were dying now and to them New York City was just as bad a place as Mississippi. The exploitation was different but it was exploitation just the same.

When Salmon and the theatre manager, two

exploitative-looking white guys, were asked if they wanted to pay the black women to have some fun, said that they didn't want the kind of fun the black women had in mind, the black women walked away to find other white men who were willing to pay for some fun. Just then, Salmon sneezed.

"You're catching cold," said the manager.

Salmon said that his goal at that moment was to find a cheap hotel to stay in. The manager said that his goal was to get the subway station without being robbed. The two men walked along together, relieved that if a bad guy came long to victimize them, they had plenty of room in which to run.

The manager said he had a wife and two children. He had spent years working as an engineer until the company he worked for collapsed and no other companies had much use for engineers his age, so he ended up managing a porn theatre.

"Hard luck," said Salmon. Then he looked behind him and saw a white Cadillac climbing up onto the sidewalk.

?

Salmon woke up underneath a bridge with his pants down and money gone. Presently a police patrol vehicle arrived and pointed its spotlight on him as he pulled up his pants. The police thought he was another old man masturbating and defecating in public.

?

The physician at the hospital decided that Salmon was not seriously injured. The cops took him away and questioned him. He just kept telling them that he had been kidnapped by weird creatures in a Cadillac.

"I don't know who or what they were. Maybe they were from that movie, *E.T. the Extraterrestrial.*"
Salmon expressed himself with much innocence, but his remark began an epidemic of mind-poisoning. Here is how it spread: A reporter from the New York *Post* used Salmon's quote:

### E.T. BANDITS
### VICTIMIZE PAIR

They gave Salmon's name as Sal Willis, address unknown. They listed his age as ninety-one.

Other newspapers copied the story and tweaked it as they pleased. They all loved the joke about E.T. and spoke of *The E.T. Gang* as if it were real. Reporters started asking police for information on *The E.T. Gang*, so the police started seeking information on *The E.T. Gang*.

?

So New Yorkers had something new to fear, a tangible new thing called *The E.T. Gang*. They bought new locks for their doors and had broken windows fixed. They were afraid to go out at night out of fear of *The E.T. Gang*.

Foreign newspapers ran stories about the new threat to public safety and advised potential travelers to limit themselves to a few street so that the tourists wouldn't be victimized by *The E.T. Gang*.

?

In a Manhattan ghetto, a dozen dark-skinned group of boys, knowing that everyone seemed to fear *The E.T. Gang*, decided to create or join that gang. One of them, a good painter, painted an image of the movie character E.T. on the backs of their leather jackets.

# 9

While Willard Salmon caused much damage in New York City, Centric Cline, getting sicker every day in Vancouver, wandered about the Best Western hotel of which he was part owner.

He ended up in the carpeted, fresh-smelling lobby and wanted to check in and get a room. Even though it was four in the morning, someone else was checking in, too. That person was brown. He was Jaz Johal, the young doctor from India, and he wanted to stay at the Best Western until he could find a comfortable apartment somewhere close to the hospital.

Centrick stood in line, quiet and modest. He believed that his status as part-owner of the hotel did not entitle him to special treatment. He also believed he should feel O.K. about staying in a place where Indian men stayed. "If it's good enough for him, it's good enough for me," he muttered to himself.

?

The desk clerk was so new that he had no idea who Centrick Cline was, even though Centrick's name stood, huge and blazing, on the sign right next door. He asked Centrick to fill out the registration form, and when Centrick did as asked and handed it back, he felt a sense of quite significant achievement. He beamed as the night man handed him the room key, and he fell in love with his room as soon as he entered it. The room, he told himself, was fresh and lovely, just like ten zillion other Best Western rooms.

"I won't get sick in here," he said aloud as he collapsed onto the bed. Getting sick with some dreadful disease was very much on his mind most of the time. He especially feared AIDS; he feared that people would think he was a homosexual if he died that way.

He got naked and lay back, smiling because he knew that the AIDS virus, called Human Immunodeficiency Virus (HIV) was not airborne.

Yet.

# 10

Willard Salmon stayed in the New York City Police Departmnet building until they were convinced he no longer represented a clear and present danger to the people of that city. They released him—in the middle of the night. He left the premises and walked around town with no particular destination in mind.

He wandered over to the Lincoln Tunnel, where he hitched a ride and got into a truck that was hauling a huge load of something. Salmon knew that the tunnel was named for an American president who had had the courage and imagination to make human slavery illegal in the United States of America.

Those slaves were let loose without any land or money or food or other resources. They were simply told to get lost. They were easy to spot because they were black. They were now free simply to fend for themselves.

?

The driver, who was white, told Salmon that he would have to sit on the floor of the cab because picking up hitchhikers could get the driver into big trouble.

?

Later, the driver told him to sit up. They had reached New Jersey by then. As they passed the poisoned meadows and marshes, the driver told Salmon that he had been a hunter and fisherman years earlier. He said it was tragic how the places he'd hunted and fished in had deteriorated. "It's all factories now and all they make is shit like pet food, soda, candy bars—"

?

Salmon nodded; the driver was right. The manufacturing process had destroyed America, and most of what was being manufactured was shit.

"Martha Stewart is polishing the brass on the

Titanic," said Salmon. "The whole shithole is coming down, and I say good riddance to life as we've known it. Maybe the civilization that replaces ours will be a better one."

The driver scowled. "I hope you're kidding."

"Not at all."

"Maybe you're right."

"I'm *always* right."

?

They rode on in silence for a while. Then the driver said, "I see now that my truck pollutes the environment. I suppose I'm committing slow suicide."

"No big deal," said Salmon. "You're better off dead."

"Years ago my brother worked for a defense contractor. His job was to make Agent Orange for use in Vietnam." Vietnam was a country far away. Uncle Sam wanted to kill off the communists in Vietnam who were trying to take over the whole country, The method Uncle Sam used was to drop bombs on the country to kill all the communists. He hired men to make Agent Orange, a chemical that eliminated the foliage so the men in airplanes would have an easier time finding the commies who were hiding in the foliage.

"The commies won anyway despite Agent Orange," said Salmon.

?

"You're putting me on," said the driver. "I'm not sure of you're serious or you're putting me on."

"I'm always serious, except when I'm putting people on," said Salmon. He added, "Life is much too important to be taken seriously."

?

Salmon would later become very famous and one of the things people asked was, "How do we know when he's putting us on?"

He told them that he always crossed his toes when he was putting people on.

Salmon was a huge pain in people's asses in many ways. Soon the truck driver got sick of him and they said very little. But then they got hungry and pulled into a truckstop diner. When the driver failed to say, "Do you have money so that when the waitress brings the check you can pay for what you've eaten?" Salmon surmised that the driver was going to pay for them both.

Not far from them, a retard was having lunch too. He was a white male and the nurse helping him was a white female. He masticated his food with epic messiness. Salmon wondered how much they paid that nurse to do that awful job. It wasn't enough.

Salmon shook his head and said, "It isn't enough."

?

"I gotta take a piss," the driver said to Salmon.

"Don't let me stop you," replied Salmon.

As soon as the truck driver took his piss, the two men went back out to the parking lot. Willard Salmon got his first good look at the truck. It was huge and had PINNACLE written on its side in huge orange letters. Salmon figured that a child reading the letters would think that the truck was very important because those letters were so huge.

# 11

Centrick Cline slept until almost noon at the new Best Western. He felt profoundly refreshed. He went downstairs and ate Grand Canadian Breakfast #6 in the hotel's popular dining room, the Maple Leaf Room. At night they drew the drapes, but they were wide open now, to let the sunshine fill the room.

At the next table sat Jaz Johal, the young Indian doctor. He sat typing away on his laptop computer, searching for a cheap place to stay. Vancouver City Hospital was paying his rent for the time being, and they were getting sick of his freeloading.

He needed a girlfriend, too, or several girlfriends who would fuck and suck him whenever he wanted it, and he wanted it most of the time. He also wished to be back with his Indian relatives. He knew a few hundred of them by name.

Johal's face showed no expression as he

ordered Grand Canadian Breakfast #3. Behind his poker face was a young man with an excruciating case of nostalgia and horniness.

?

At the next table, Centrick Cline gazed out at vast, bustling Kingsway Street. He smiled; he knew where he was. If he got onto Kingsway and headed east, he would reach the TransCanada Highway and from there he could travel the length of Canada. If he went west he would reach the University of British Columbia and Strait of Georgia.

The University of British Columbia was where they had built the Barry Doyle Centre for the Literary Arts. Barry Doyle, a local rich guy, had donated a pile of money to the U. if they promised to build the facility and name it for him. They said yes. The literary festival would be held at that facility and would start that evening.

Centrick nodded and said the name of the huge school that had been there forever: "Yoo-bee-see."

?

Centrick swallowed the last of his breakfast and tried to convince himself that his mental illness had been cured by a good night's sleep and a substantial, sensible breakfast.

His mental illness allowed him to walk across the lobby and into the lounge without flipping out. But as soon as he left the lounge and entered the sidewalk, he felt as if his legs had turned to rubber.

?

He made it across to his truck dealership. There he spotted a young Native man who was polishing a Ford F-150 with a rag. The young man looked at Centrick and smiled. His smile was amazingly white.

The young Native man had just been paroled from Rainford Prison. He needed a job right away so that he would not starve to death. So there he was, polishing a truck so that Centrick Cline would see how hard a worker he was.

From age nine, he had spent nearly all of his life in youth shelters, jails and orphanages and foster homes. He was now twenty-seven.

?

But he was now free!

?

Centrick wasn't sure that the young Native man actually existed.

?

The Native man went back to polishing the truck. He believed most of the time that life, or at least *his* life, was not worth living. He had little idea of how to live a good and proper life and he looked forward to dying. He thought the world was an awful place and that he should not have been born. He had no friends or relatives. He had simply gone from one cage to another.

He often thought of a better world and had a name for it. He kept the name all to himself, because he felt that if he shared it with anyone it wouldn't be

*his* any longer. The name of that better world was
PARADISE.

?

He had a picture of Centrick in his wallet. In prison
he had listened to the truck dealer's radio ads
countless times. The main message was always the
same: "You have a friend on Kingsway Street." The
Native man had an easy time convincing himself that
he and Centrick Cline were friends and that Centrick
might help him out by giving him a job. The Native
man decided that if Centrick Cline gave him a job, it
would be the same thing as being in paradise.

"Sir," said the Native man, "I am a very hard
worker and I understand that you are a truly excellent
employer. I believe I was meant to work for you."

"How's that?" asked Centrick Cline.

"It's just a feeling I have. My name is Billy Pope."

Billy Pope was a very common Native name
around Vancouver.

?

Centrick Cline shook his head and walked away. Billy Pope nearly cried.

Centrick Cline went into his showroom and noticed that his legs no longer felt rubbery. His problem now was that a palm tree seemed to be growing out of his showroom floor. His mental illness had forgotten all about Aloha Week. He himself had designed the palm tree he now beheld. It now freaked him out a lot, especially when he saw the coconuts and ukuleles everywhere.

Then he saw something truly amazing: His sales manager, Harri Singh, stood before him in a lime-green leotard with a grass skirt.

?

Harri and his wife had spent the entire weekend wondering if Centrick suspected that Harri was a transvestite. They finally agreed that Centrick had no reason to suspect such a thing. Harri had never spoken to Centrick about women's clothing. He had never entered a transvestite beauty contest nor joined the big transvestites' club in downtown Vancouver.

He had never visited the city's transvestite nightclub, Eve's and had never visited any trans Website.

Harri and his wife assured themselves, and each other, that Centrick simply meant that Harri had better put on some goofy Hawaiian clothes if he wished to remain employed.

So Harri stood before Centrick, scared and exhilarated and feeling wonderful and liberated.

"Aloha," he said to Centrick.

# 12

Willard Salmon got closer to Centrick Cline but was still far, far away. The truck named *Pinnacle* barreled on down the highway.

"Were you in the military?" asked Willard Salmon, just to make conversation.

"Nope," replied the driver. "You're a little bit older than I am. Did you fight in Vietnam?"

"I'm Canadian," said Salmon. "I couldn't have fought in that war if I wanted to."

The driver said that at one time in his life he had more friends than he could count. As a truck driver, he was on the road most of the time and most of his friends had found other friends and stopped considering *him* their friend.

"In your work, you have contacts, don't you?" the driver asked him. "You have friends. You play cards, drink beer, have a few laughs. Am I right?"

"I'm older than they are. We don't have much in common," replied Salmon.

"You have a routine," said the driver. "You know people, you see them every day. My whole life happens in this truck. The conversations I have are with waitresses at truck stops."

Salmon shrugged and muttered.

The driver convinced himself that Salmon had a wide circle of friends. Then, for his own amusement, he pretended that Salmon had asked him about the sex life of an American coast-to-coast truck driver. Salmon could not have cared less.

"You want to know how I make out with the women, right? You have this notion that I'm banging bitches from New York to L.A., right?"

"I guess."

"Well, Willard—that's your name, right?"

"Yes."

"Well, Willard, if my truck broke down, how easy do you think it would be for me to get laid, looking as scruffy as I do?"

"That depends on how much you *wanted* to get

laid," said Willard.

The driver sighed. "Yeah, you're probably right. That's the story of my life:  Didn't want anything badly enough." Then, "You married, Willard?"

"I've been married three times." He was telling the truth. All three of his wives had been patient, wonderful women. Each had left him after discovering that she could not help him overcome his pessimism.

"Any children?"

"One. He's a man now. I have no idea where he is. Just as well, I guess."

?

Salmon's son ran away from home at age fourteen, lied about his age and joined the Canadian Armed Forces. He sent a note to his father: "How does it feel to be such an *asshole*?"

The next time the son's name came up, it happened because the Canadian authorities visited Salmon to tell him that his son had deserted his unit overseas and joined an armed settlement on the West

Bank.

Here is what the Canadian authorities had to say about Salmon's son: "Your boy sure is in big trouble."

# 13

When Centrick Cline saw Harri Singh dressed in a lime-green leotard and grass skirt, he felt so ashamed and embarrassed that he ducked into his office and forced himself to think of other things.

Agnes Semko, his secretary, came in looking normal expect for a lei of flowers around her neck. She absolutely adored her boss and thought Aloha Week a grand idea.

"Isn't this *fun*?" she asked, beaming.

"I'm not well. Let Harri handle the sales and you handle running this place. Keep all weirdoes away from me."

"The twins are here," said Agnes. "Something bad is happening at the miniature golf course."

Centrick was grateful for a simple, clear message that he could deal with. The twins were his stepbrothers, Eric and Derek Cline. They owned the Great Pacific Miniature Golf Course, a highly popular tourist trap not far north of the Canadian border. The golf course was the twins' only source of income; they resided in small houses near the golf course.

?

Eric and Derek sat on the leather sofa while they waited for Centrick. Often he had much difficulty telling them apart. As children, they used to complete each other's sentences and had their own verbal shorthand that was incomprehensible to everyone else.

Here is how Centrick and the twins had come to be related to each other: Centrick had been adopted by the Clines; not long after that, the Clines, who had tried for years without success to have children, conceived twin boys. Looking at them now, Centrick felt pleased to have them at his workplace, these two short, fat men in their overalls and porkpie hats reminded him of who he was. Centrick brought them in and closed the door. "O.K., what's happening at the golf course—?"

"Too many gangs," said Derek.

Centrick nodded. Lately members of the rival

meth gangs had started hanging out there to unwind after a busy day of making money and eluding the cops. "Do they fight?"

"No, they're just *there* and they scare people away."

"Don't start worrying about it till they start beating the shit out of each other," said Centrick.

# 14

The truck carrying Willard Salmon had entered West Virginia. Much of the state had been destroyed by men and their machines in order for the land to give up its coal.

The driver said, "I saw this show on TV. It was about cobras in India. There was this little girl who, on her way home, was bitten by a cobra. She survived and had the bite mark on her arm for the rest of her life to prove she'd been bitten. People were saying, 'She's a miraculous little girl for having survived that bite. She will get preferential treatment for the rest of her life!' Other people said, 'Have you ever heard of a dry bite? Those things happen, you know.' The Indians don't seem to understand very much."

"Well," said Salmon, "I live in Vancouver, a city with lots of people from India, and they seem to own the whole fuckin' city, so they apparently understand a great deal."

# 15

Centrick Cline felt O.K. after having lunch. He remembered about Aloha Week and flowered shirts. He looked at the huge sign advertising his car dealership and understood that it was *his*; he also looked at the Best Western sign and acknowledged to himself that some of that was his, too.

He had driven to lunch in a Ford F150 truck. He drove down Kingsway Street to a restaurant called White Spot, which was one of his favorite eating places. He had read that White Spot, founded decades earlier, was so named because its preferred customers were white people. Colored folks could eat there too, maybe, way back then, but it was perfectly O.K. for them to refuse service to non-whites. On his drive back to the dealership, he turned on the radio and heard one of his own commercials: "Remember, you have a friend on Kingsway."

Although his White Spot lunch had revived him,

he still felt mentally ill. He began repeating what he heard on the radio. So when the radio pitchman said, "Remember, you have a friend on Kingsway," Centrick said, "Kingsway." He did that with all the commercials, knowing it was involuntary and grateful that no one was around to hear him carry on like that.

?

Back at the truck dealership, the Native ex-convict Bill Parry loitered. His big goal in life was to work for the legendary Vancouver businessman Centrick Cline. But Centrick did not want Parry on his property, and instructed his employees to chase him off. As soon as he saw a Centrick Cline employee approaching, Bill would hurry over to the Best Western and stare at the debris dumpster until the employee went away. Then Bill would sneak back to the truck dealership, eager to spot the boss.

The actual Centrick Cline by that time had become so mentally unstable that he often believed he was *not* Centrick Cline. Who *was* he? He often didn't know, and his ignorance troubled him. When the boss arrived at the huge lot on Kingsway, Bill said, "You sure you're not Mr. Cline?" When Centrick replied, "I'm not Centrick Cline," Bill said, "Sure coulda fooled me."

?

Centrick had a cheeseburger, fries, a side of gravy, coleslaw and a pop at White Spot. The restaurant was located on Kingsway Street, a dozen blocks from the truck dealership. Not far from White Spot, a new high school was under construction. They were going to name it Pierre Elliot Trudeau Secondary School, in honor of the late Canadian prime minister who had once made an obscene finger gesture at some Canadian photojournalists. Centrick couldn't remember the last time Trudeau had visited Canada, but he knew that Trudeau had died of natural causes. He also knew that sometimes American presidents were shot to death while in office, but nobody had ever tried to assassinate a Canadian prime minister. Centrick Cline wondered about that sometimes.

?

Centrick's server at White Spot was a twenty-eight-year-old woman named Ronaye Bardell. She was of medium height and build, with a very slim body and a big blonde smile. Centrick Cline thought her very pretty.

Ronaye Bardell, closing in on thirty, worked at White Spot to save up for a condominium in or near downtown Vancouver, and such condominiums cost close to half a million dollars apiece.

Centrick admired Ronaye's good looks but did not get an erection as he sat and she stood while they chatted. He wasn't sure if she knew who he was, and that his name was on that gigantic sign down the street. He was very smart, rich and successful; she was a dumb, cute Canadian chick who worked at White Spot because that was the best job she could get. If he said, "I have bigger bucks than you could earn in ten lifetimes. Help me spend some of my money," would she say, "O.K."?

Ronaye Bardell was dumb because she needed to be. In Vancouver, being an intelligent woman— especially a young and pretty one—would mean that such a woman had few friends and many enemies. The idea was to make everyone think she was a cute, dumb chick; maybe then some rich guy would come along and offer her a much better life than the one she had been burdened with.

?

Ronaye knew perfectly well who Centrick was, and it didn't matter if *he* knew who *she* was because *he* mattered and *she* didn't. As she stood there talking to him, her heart pounded, her nipples hardened and her vagina lubricated—all because he had most of the things she wanted in life. With the greatest of ease, he could solve most or all of her problems. He could move her into his fine house and put her in the driver's seat of a fancy car and keep her pockets full of walking-around money so that she would never have to work another shift at White Spot.

Ronaye said, "If you don't mind my saying so, Mr. Cline, I want to congratulate you on all the success you've had. I see your name in lights all the way down the street and I hear your commercials on the radio. Whenever you come in, everyone around here is just *amazed*."

"Amazed," said Centrick. That was his mental illness manifesting itself again.

?

"Maybe I chose the wrong word," Ronaye said, blushing. She often said she was sorry for using words the wrong way. At school they'd told her not to be shy about apologizing for using language poorly. In Vancouver, most white people were like that— inarticulate and illiterate. They had poor vocabularies and kept their sentences short so that their listeners wouldn't say, "Wow! You are very inarticulate!" Centrick didn't do that because he was smarter than everyone else, but Ronaye did it because she had to.

When Ronaye was a student at Oliver Johnson Secondary School, her English teacher would mock and penalize the students whenever they used slang or mispronounced certain words. Also, she told them they were *idiots* if they couldn't understand long, dense novels like *Nicholas Nickelby* or *War and Peace*.

?

The Chinese and Indian students had parents who were pushing them towards careers in dentistry and accounting, where the money was. Those students said, "Why do I have to read *Crime and Punishment* or *David Copperfield*? What do they have to do with dentistry or accounting?"

?

Ronaye Bardell flunked English when she had to read and write a paper about a book called *Dubliners*, a short-story collection written by an Irishman named James Joyce. Some people said that James Joyce was the finest English-language fiction writer of the past two hundred years and that one of his books, *Ulysses*, was the best novel of the past two hundred years even though nobody was sure of what it was *about*.

So Ronaye flunked English. *Dubliners* was about people James Joyce knew when he was a kid, and most folks who knew about James Joyce said that *Dubliners* was the easiest Joyce book to read. So they stuck her into a remedial reading class where they made her read comic books.

During that summer she lost her virginity. She was raped by a service technician named Mike Fillo in the parking lot of the Pacific Coliseum during the Pacific National Exhibition. She refused to report it to the police or anyone else, since her father was dying at the time and she didn't want to subject herself to the ordeal of having her vagina examined and answering a bunch of personal questions.

?

As Centrick sat there and Roanye stood there and they talked to each other, he wondered how much longer his mental illness would last, and Ronaye needed to know if he would share some of what he had with her, and what he would want in return, although she assumed he wanted what all other men wanted from her, and what she had that they wanted sat on her chest and between her legs. She hoped Centrick Cline wanted those things, too.

"Well," she said to him, "I notice you come here a lot and I sure hope you think our food is yummy."

"Yummy," he said, nodding.

She chuckled. "Well, it *is* yummy, right?"

"Right."

"We serve you the same food we serve everyone else. It doesn't matter to us that you're Centrick Cline."

"Centrick Cline."

?

It mattered very little what Centrick Cline said. He had been around for so long and achieved so much that his business empire pretty much ran itself. Most of the people in Vancouver—and everywhere else— had their jobs to do and roles to play, so that most of what they said was just a bunch of noise. If the person's brain chemistry went bad and they could no longer function, they began to slip through the cracks and the help available to them, called "psychiatric care," almost always was too little and too late, so the sick person kept slipping through the cracks until they were invisible and disappeared forever.

That was why the people at Centrick Cline's Ford Trucks were slow to observe their boss's mental deterioration. They just kept convincing themselves that he still was the guy he had always been and always would be. It was easy for them to convince themselves of that.

?

Once Centrick paid for his meal and left White Spot, Ronaye believed she could make him happy with her firm, pert young breasts, fresh-smelling vagina and heart-shaped bottom. She wanted to burst into tears about the deep sad lines in his face and the fact that Mrs. Cline had killed herself with Tylenol 3s and orange juice and vodka. She knew that his dog got into fights all the time and that his son was a homosexual. She knew these things because everyone who cared to know could learn them easily enough.

She gazed into the distance and saw Grouse Mountain. She imagined the transmitter tower of CYVR, the radio station that Centrick Cline owned. The tower, which sat upon Grouse Mountain, made it possible for everyone throughout the Lower Mainland to listen to CYVR. The station itself, on Richards Street, was always a hub of activity, with lots of important people coming in and going out, and a tall tower on the roof with a blinking red light to keep aircraft away.

Ronaye Bardell scratched her chin and smiled, picturing new and used Ford trucks, all of them owned by Centrick Cline.

?

British Columbia and Washington state seismologists kept saying, "Prepare for a major earthquake in the next fifty years." The earthquake they had in mind was something like 9.0 on the Richter scale and would probably cause a *tsunami*, or harbor wave, that would cause massive damage and kill many people. The experts in Washington state said that such an earthquake would also cause nearby Mount Rainier to erupt. The catastrophe would cause tens of thousands of deaths and billions of dollars in damage.

That type of thing.

?

Centrick drove from White Spot to have a look at the construction site of the new high school. He did not want to go back to the truck dealership just yet because he was feeling mentally ill. Agnes Semko, his secretary and sex partner, could run the place just fine without any assistance from Centrick or anyone else.

He had trained her remarkably well, and the dealership mostly ran itself.

He moseyed around the construction site and wondered why the Vancouver School Board had chosen to name a school for a prime minister who had flipped off those new cameramen. He thought for a moment about Vancouver, the city in which he had spent all his life, and how it had changed, especially since 1986, when Vancouver hosted the World's Fair—they called it Expo 86. Centrick resented all the changes in the city, but supposed that he had no right to complain, especially since he was so much better off than most other Vancouverites. He shrugged and went back to his vehicle.

?

Centrick Cline forgot about Ronaye Bardell moments after leaving White Spot, but she thought about him for the rest of the day and even telephoned him. But by then he was unavailable to take her call because he had become an inpatient at Vancouver City Hospital's psychiatric ward.

But before he was locked up, he went back to the

truck dealership and hid out in his office because he was ashamed of his mental illness. After staring at a wall for ten minutes, he telephone Agnes, his secretary, who was maybe fifteen feet away. "Agnes, I need to ask you a question," he said.

"The answer is yes."

"Leave with me immediately. Let's go to the Good Night Inn in New Westminster."

?

So they did. Part of Agnes' job was to do things like that for Centrick. She found it especially important to accommodate him because he seemed so out of sorts. Only problem was, hers was the busiest desk at the busiest dealership in Greater Vancouver, and as soon as Centrick left the premises, she became the boss, not that the places really *needed* a boss. Anyway, she couldn't just bugger off because Centrick had a boner. So she went over to Barbara MacDougall, the cashier at the back of the room, and asked her to take care of things for the next little while.

"You should have a teenaged squeeze who can ride your dick whenever you get the urge," Agnes said to Centrick.

"If you can find me one, send her to my office."

Barbara didn't want to be the boss while Agnes was off riding Centrick's dick. Barbara was still recovering from the hysterectomy she'd had after having been knocked up by Mike Fillo, the guy who had raped Ronaye Bardell during the Pacific National Exhibition. Agnes, in her mid-twenties, had gone in for an abortion, which the abortionist—"the safecracker," she had called him—had botched up. Thus her hysterectomy.

"I don't want to be the boss of this lunatic asylum," she said.

But she did so anyway. "My life sucks," she said. "But I don't have the balls to commit suicide, so I may just as well try to make myself useful."

?

Centrick and Agnes drove to the Good Night Inn in separate vehicles so as to make people think they were *not* going someplace to screw, although everyone who cared to know already knew that those two were screwing.

There was practically nothing that Agnes would refuse to do for Centrick. She was absolutely supportive of him in every way, and he appreciated her loyalty. As they drove out to New Westminster that day to screw, he hoped he would give her a lay she would remember fondly for many years.

?

Willard Salmon once wrote a novel about sex because one of his wives told him that there was money to be made in the writing of erotic novels. So he did as told.

He wrote a novel about a talking vagina.

?

Centrick and Agnes had sexual intercourse in the Good Night Inn. Then they remained in bed for a while. Both people had beautiful bodies, and they knew it.

"That was our first time in the afternoon," said Centrick. "I was full of anxiety."

"You needed this."

"Yes." He lay naked on his back. His big cock slept. He felt proud of his big cock, his beautiful body, his wealth and business success. Sometimes, he had to admit, it was a good thing to be Centrick Cline.

Agnes Semko, a woman whose metabolism kept her svelte and therefore attractive to men, was paid only slightly more than minimum wage by Centrick Cline. Her husband, Bart Semko, had been killed in Afghanistan. A career officer in the Canadian Armed Forces, he had been shot to death by terrorists who resented his presence in their country.

?

Agnes followed Bart from coast to coast as his military career progressed. At one point they moved to Toronto so that he could get a master's degree in sociology at the taxpayers' expense.

After that, she went with him to Chilliwack, which was near Vancouver, so that he could be an instructor at a military base.

They moved closer to Vancouver because they found Chilliwack insufferably boring. Agnes took a job at Centrick Cline Ford Trucks, if only to bring in some money and combat boredom.

But then they sent Bart to Afghanistan.

Soon after that, Centrick Cline's wife killed herself with Tylenol 3s and orange juice and vodka and Bart Semko came home in a body bag.

?

"You men have it rough," she said as they lay in bed in the Good Night Inn. "You have to be tough even when you feel weak and vulnerable."

She looked at the window and pictured Rainford Prison somewhere in the distance. The prison had nearly all white guards and the prisoners were mostly Natives and Indians. "I've heard that nobody ever escapes from Rainford," she said to Centrick.

"Nobody ever tries," he told her.

?

"Know what?" Agnes said to Centrick.

"What?"

"I was just thinking that this would be a great location for a Tim Hortons." Tim Hortons was a donut shop that was immensely popular in Canada.

Centrick tensed up immediately. The reason for his tension was that he wanted her to love him for who he was, not for what he had. It sounded to him as if she wanted him to buy her a Tim Hortons out there on Kingsway Street.

?

Agnes, who had been so proud of her ability to keep Centrick relaxed, now watched him tighten up. "What's wrong? Why are you so tight now?"

"If you're going to ask me for goodies, just make damn sure that you don't start asking right after we've had sex. Sex and goodies need to be dealt with separately. Understand?"

"I'm not sure I know what you're talking about," she said.

He contorted his face and said, in a mock-female voice, "I'm not sure I know what you're talking about."

?

Agnes got out of bed, offended that he would speak to her in such a way. "*I* don't speak to *you* that way," she said aloud. Centrick snarled at her and said that women were whores, including Agnes, and when Agnes said she wanted a Tim Hortons franchise, she was proving to him that he was right. He said that such a business would cost well over a hundred thousand dollars, when all expenses were determined.

Agnes burst into tears, and after collecting herself sufficiently, she told him that she wanted the Tim Hortons restaurant for *him*, and that her main goal in life was to make him happy.

"I've noticed that so many people who come out this way are heading to Rainford Prison to visit their relatives, and that most of those people are poor, and you know how much poor people love junk food, and Tim Hortons mostly sells donuts and coffee, which are the most popular kinds of junk food."

"So you want me to open a junk-food joint for poor people?"

"Harri Singh was right about you."

"Harri Singh is a goof."

# 17

Blondie Cline, Centrick's homosexual son, began dressing for work. His job was to play piano in the cocktail lounge of the Best Western hotel next door to the Ford truck dealership. He was indigent; he lived in a smelly, poorly furnished room at the Balmoral Hotel, a flophouse near the corner of Main and Hastings streets.

Presently Blondie Cline would be severely wounded by Centrick Cline and share an ambulance ride with Willard Salmon.

?

Blondie Cline was pale, nearly as white as an albino. He eschewed sunshine and ate only fruits and vegetables.

He did without most kinds of foods and most kinds of living things, too—he had no friends or lovers or pets. He had once been the most popular boy around. When he was a senior at the Royal Canadian Military Academy, the student body had unanimously voted him Honour Cadet, the highest rank possible.

?

While he played piano at the Best Western, Blondie had countless secrets. One of them was his invisibility. He could make it so he wasn't there. Blondie, in fact, disappeared from Earth entirely. He did so through Transcendental Meditation, a technique he learned from Maharishi Mahesh Yogi when the holy man visited Vancouver as part of a world tour.

The maharishi, in return for some goodies—a piece of fruit, a bunch of flowers and fifty dollars in cash—taught Blondie to transport himself far, far away by chanting, "Mmmmm mmmm mmmm."

?

Blondie did TM while sitting on the foot of his bed. Afterwards he felt better because he had ceased being Blondie Cline for a few minutes. He got up and brushed his military crewcut for a moment or two.

?

Blondie was sent away to military school so that, in Centrick's words, they would "beat the faggot out of him." Blondie at age ten told his father, "Daddy, I want to be a girl. You're rich, so is there I doctor you can send me to who will make me into a girl?"

?

Check this out: Blondie Cline at age ten was sent to Royal Canadian Military Academy for eight years of athletics, homosexuality and homicide. The boys were taught to stay in the best possible physical condition so they could quickly and unemotionally kill the "enemy." They would be taught, when the time was right, who the "enemy" was. They were not to ask why the "enemy" was bad or why the "enemy" should be killed.

Blondie did it all without much effort. He brought home medals to show his parents. He had learned to fence, fox, wrestle and swim. He could shoot a variety of firearms and hit any number of targets. He could drive all manner of motor vehicles and ride horses.

He showed his medals to his parents, knowing that those medals didn't matter very much. What his parents wanted was for the military academy to "beat the faggot" out of Blondie, which did not happen. On most days he very much enjoyed shoving his big cock into the other boys and having them shoving theirs into him, too.

His mother indicated to him that she was very unhappy. She hinted to her son that Centrick was the reason for her unhappiness. She was wrong; her mental illness was the reason for her unhappiness.

"The thing I can't stand about him is"—but then she would shake her head and not say anything more. "You're too young and innocent to hear this," she would say at other times, even when he was the toughest, coldest, meanest sixteen-year-old in Canada. "I have secrets that I will never tell *anyone*."

Among her secrets, of course, was one that she kept to herself right up until she offed herself with Tylenol 3s and vodka. She had a huge monkey on her back.

My mother did, too.

?

Here's the deal: Blondie's mother and my mother were very different kinds of people. But they were both beautiful and full of talk about how shitty life was. Both women were profoundly pessimistic and I suppose they had a right to feel that way. Also, our mothers committed suicide. His did so with pills and booze and mine ate herself to death. Nice work if you can get it.

?

At least Blondie Cline'a mother taught him to play piano. By doing so she gave him a marketable skill for life; he could go anywhere and everywhere and make a living as a pianist, and Blondie was an especially gifted player. His military training had prepared him for very little. The Canadian Armed Forces knew he was a homosexual who would inevitably fall in love with other men in the service, so the military had no use for him.

?

So Blondie Cline got ready for work. He put on a black turtleneck sweater and a black dinner jacket. He looked out his room's only window, which was streaked with filth. It looked out onto nothing; the better rooms had views of the rest of downtown.

Blondie's part of town was called skid row. He had been there all his life and skid row was where most of Vancouver's Natives lived, and some of the Native women worked as prostitutes there. They called that neighborhood the Downtown East Side. Over the years, a local pig farmer had driven into skid row and said to the local whores, many of whom were Natives, "Hey, girls! Come back to my pig farm and we'll party!" Some of them did. When they got to his pig farm, he killed them and inserted their bodies into his wood-chipper, then he fed their ground-up remains to his pigs. He got away with it for the longest time, mostly because the whore would be gone from her Downtown East Side home for days or weeks or months before anyone noticed her absence. Those disappearances happened so many times that the cops started asking questions, and the people they questioned said that smelly white pig farmer was always hanging out in those skid-row bars and offering to buy drinks for Native whores, so maybe he had something to do with it.

The cops raided that pig farm and charged its owner with murder because they found bits and pieces of the women who had been reported missing. They put him in prison and he's still there, mumbling to himself.

?

Blondie Cline looked in his filthy mirror and said what the American president Barack Obama had taught America to say.

"Yes I can," he said. "Yes I can."

# 18

The truck Willard Salmon was riding in neared Vancouver but they were caught in bumper-to-bumper traffic. So everyone just had to sit there and be patient.

?

Years later, when Willard Salmon was a very, very old man, a psychiatrist asked him if he feared the future.

"Doc," he said, "it's the *past* that freaks *me* out."

?

Not more than a few kilometres from Willard Salmon, Centrick Cline sat in the dark, quiet cocktail lounge of the Best Western. The place was fairly cool, too, and it was easy to forget all about the insane Kingsway Street traffic outside.

?

Blondie Cline sat playing the piano in the dark, cool, quiet cocktail lounge. When Centrick Cline entered the room, neither man acknowledge the other one in any way. They had been estranged for years.

?

Check this out: Agnes Semko sat in the Ford dealership next door, catching up on all the business she had been unable to do while having sexual intercourse with Centrick at the Good Night Inn. Centrick would punch her out presently.

The only person on the property with her at that moment was Billy Pope, the Native ex-convict. He wandered among the rows of used trucks. Centrick would try to punch him out, too, but Billy was too good a fighter to be beaten up by Centrick.

Agnes worked like hell, doing this and that as fast as she could.

Billy Pope, however, had nothing to do. He wished he could be busy and useful like Agnes. He wanted to get into one of the trucks and sit there for a while but they were all locked. So he stood there and for a time stared at the Canadian flag as it flapped in the breeze. Centrick had had the flagpole installed and a huge maple-leaf flag added to it so that people who visited his dealership would remember which country they were in.

Billy Pope put his hand over his heart and said, "O Canada. My home and native land."

?

Billy Pope spent some time looking at the ungodly Kingsway Street traffic. "Time for people to go home," he said, nodding. He stood there watching it till it thinned out. "Most people home now."

The sun went down and he felt cold. He wondered if he would die of exposure that night. He had no idea how that would feel because he had spent most of his life for the past while indoors. But he listened to the radio often and heard the announcers say that people caught in the outdoors overnight died of exposure.

He missed the indoors and the sound of the radio. He liked eating, sleeping and listening to the radio as a way of life. He missed a lifestyle of doing very, very little. He enjoyed shoving his cock into other men's orifices and having the same done to him. He liked fucking the cows in the prison dairy, too.

?

He kept his hand over his heart as he looked up at the Canadian flag. He smiled, revealing a mouthful of ivory-bright teeth. Rainford Prison was very proud of its dental program.

That program had become so famous that it had been written up in many health and general-readership magazines. Rainford Prison began its dental program out of the belief that ex-convicts could not get good jobs if they had bad teeth.

The joke went that, even in neighboring provinces like Alberta and Saskatchewan, whenever the cops picked up someone with especially good-looking teeth, the cop would say, "O.K., guy, how much time did you do in Rainford?"

?

Billy Pope wandered into the Best Western's cocktail

lounge and heard the server call out to the bartender, "Vodka and orange." He had no clue as to what that meant, any more than he understand what a Long Island Iced Tea was, or a Labatt's Blue, or a Tom Collins or a Rob Roy. "I need a Southern Comfort over ice," or a White Russian.

Billy's only experience with alcohol had to do with drinking Listerine or cooking wine. He had no interest in beer, wine or other alcoholic beverages.

?

"Give me a Coors on tap," he heard the server say, and Billy should have paid special attention to that. That beverage wasn't for just anyone; it was for the person who had created Billy and all his misery, the person who could make him a zillionaire or a quadriplegic. That person was me.

?

I had come to this festival for one reason: To watch a confrontation between Willard Salmon and Centrick Cline.

"This book you're writing? It's not so good," I

said to myself.

"Not so bad, either."

"You're afraid maybe you'll kill yourself the way your mother did."

"I won't eat myself to death. I don't like food that much."

I have had lifelong problems with anxiety and depression. But I feel better now.

Truth be told: I feel much better now.

?

I sat there in the Kingsway Street Best Western hotel that existed only in my imagination. I made up a cocktail server and named her Bonnie Picard. I decided that she and Centrick Cline had known each other for years. Her husband worked as a guard at Rainford Prison. She had to work because he had lost all their money by investing in an upscale men's clothing store located at Granville Street and 16th Avenue in Vancouver. The store sold only Italian clothing made in Milan. Vancouver men did not spend $200 for a pair of slacks. Their women did not spend that kind of money on slacks for their men.

The store lost piles of the Picards' money from day one.

Centrick had advised them against investing in that clothing store. He knew Bonnie and her husband because they had bought Ford trucks from him.

"We love Ford trucks," they had told him.

?

As he sat in the cocktail lounge, Centrick reminded himself that the Literary Arts Festival at the Barry Doyle Centre was about to begin at the University of British Columbia and that most of the guests were staying at the Best Western out on Kingsway Street, which was some distance from the University of British Columbia campus. Still, he hoped that some of those people would join him in the cocktail lounge; he wanted to meet them and find out if they had any insights into life or the human condition that he had missed. He wanted someone to tell him something that would enable him to laugh at his own misfortunes; to continue living; and to stay out of the psychiatric wing at Vancouver City Hospital, which was where the "acute" cases went.

?

Centrick, so open to new ways of thinking and living that he just stared ahead and wished he was someone and somewhere else, was oblivious to two distinguished people who entered the cocktail lounge and sat at Blondie's piano. They were Kiesha Beeman, a feminist novelist, and Kara Rebokian, the abstract painter.

Blondie's piano, a Steinway grand, was big enough to accommodate over a half-dozen people, and guests were free to sit at its sides and eat or drink while enjoying Blondie's music.

?

"This place is awful," said Kara Rebokian. "Just awful."

Kiesha Beeman, the feminist novelist, had been born and raised in Vancouver but made enough money to leave many years earlier. "I was terrified about coming back here after all this time," she said.

"Canadians are always afraid of coming home," said Kara. "Canada is a very easy place to outgrow."

"All Canadians outgrow Canada. If you're a Canadian, it helps to have a sense of humor because Canada is such a joke."

?

About a kilometre east of the Best Western, traffic on Kingsway slowed to practically nothing because of a fatal crash. Drivers and their passengers got out of their vehicles and stretched their legs as they peered into the distance to see what the problem was up ahead.

# 21

Willard Salmon entered the cocktail lounge. His feet felt hot. He wanted to remove his shoes and socks and hold his feet up to an air conditioner, which always helped cool him off. Whenever he stayed in a hotel or motel and his room had air conditioning, he liked to turn it on full blast and leave it that way all day and night; something about having frigid air blowing on him made him feel very sleepy. But he walked in now, his feet very hot.

Kara Rebokian and Kiesha Beeman did not see him come in. Some other attendees from the Literary Arts Festival had come by to say hello and they all gathered by the piano to visit while Blondie played for them. Rebokian's speech had been greeted with cheers and applause. Everyone said now that Vancouver had one of the world's finest paintings.

"You explained it to me," said Bonnie Picard.

"You made me understand."

"I didn't know my work needed to be explained," said Marco Carloni as he shrugged. "But I guess there was."

Cody Abrams, the jeweler, said, "If more artists explained their art, more people would become more interested in it."

That type of thing.

Willard Salmon was feeling freaked out. he thought that maybe people would greet him as physically and noisily as Maurice Milos had done, and Salmon had no idea of how to deal with that. But Maurice stayed out of his way and sat near Centrick Cline and me instead.

Centrick Cline remained oblivious to the goings on in that cocktail lounge. He stared straight ahead, seeing nothing. Then he started moving his lips and what came out was, "Mmmmm mmmm mmmm."

?

Willard Salmon had a thick manila envelope containing a number of documents including a copy of his book *What the Man Doesn't Want You to Know.*

This book contained many pornographic pictures plus the story that Centrick Cline would take much too seriously.

So the three of us sat there in the cocktail lounge without much to say to each other, although Willard Salmon was about to drive Centrick bonkers and Centrick was about to bite Salmon as hard as he could.

Billy Pope checked us out through a kitchen peephole until a man tapped him on the shoulder and said, "You've been fed. Now leave."

So Billy nodded and wandered outside. Soon he stood among Centrick's used trucks again. He started muttering to himself again.

?

In the cocktail lounge, the bartender switched on the fluorescent overhead lights and his vest immediately became ridiculously shiny because it was made partly of fluorescent material that lit up when under fluorescent light. The same thing happened to Bonnie Picard's uniform.

Willard Salmon did not understand why those

uniforms suddenly became incandescent. Like most other science fiction writers, his work was far more fiction than science.

Centrick Cline now became mesmerized by Bonnie Picard's uniform, much as he became mesmerized by many things these days. He now thought about something his father had told him years earlier: Some business succeed while others fail.

Bonnie Picard had to wait tables because her husband had lost all their money by financing a men's store on Granville Street. The main reason so many Vancouver men's stores had failed was that they were in bad locations—Robson Street would have been a far better choice—and that the people who bought high-end men's clothes—rich Chinese guys and their wives—recognized $20 shirts that had been marked up to $200 as ripoffs.

"If you put the wrong business in the wrong part of town," said Centrick Cline's father, "you will lose one hundred percent of the time."

?

Willard Salmon watched as Centrick stared out at

nothing in particular. Salmon was aware of me, as well, even though he was looking elsewhere. I made him supremely uneasy. That was because he was the only character I had ever created who knew that he had been created by another human being. He had spoken several times about it to his bird. "Seriously, Kit, sometimes I think I'm just a character in someone else's book and that writer is saying, 'I wonder how I can torture him today.'"

Now Salmon nodded, knowing he was sitting in the same room as the man who had created him. He had no idea of how to react to such a realization, mainly because his reactions would be whatever I wanted them to be.

He avoided making eye contact with Centrick or me, so he dug into his manila envelope and perused its contents.

# 24

Check this out: Centrick Cline injured so many people so severely that the 911 dispatcher sent over *Veronica* to care for the victims. *Veronica*, a Greyhound-style bus, had had all of its seats removed. It held enough beds for thirty-six very unlucky people as well as a bathroom and operating room. It had enough food and medical supplies to be its own little hospital for two weeks or so.

Officially they called it the Veronica Braithwaite Memorial Mobile Disaster Unit, named for the wife of Max Braithwaite, the British Columbia Minister of Public Safety. She had died of AIDS following a blood transfusion. The "opportunistic infection" that ended her life, *pneumocystis carinii pneumonia*, or PCP made her feel as if she were drowning.

Max and Centrick bonded for a while because

they had lost their wives in strange ways within a month of each other.

The two men bought a parcel of land together out in the Fraser Valley, and as they talked to each other what to do with it, a developer came along and offered them several times the amount they had paid for it, so they sold it and divided the profits. After that, their friendship, such as it was, slowly ended because they had very little else left in common. But they still exchanged Christmas cards.

?

My psychiatrist is also named Veronica. She meets with me and other worriers once each week. It's way too much fun. She says, "I'm going to teach you to comfort others intelligently." She's gone on vacation for a month. I really like her. She's lots of fun.

I am in my fifties now and think of Jack Kerouac, whom I have now outlived. He died at age forty-seven. He drank himself to death, and towards the end of his life he published a novel called *On the Road*, which made the Beat Generation famous. The world demanded that he define Beat, but he was too dissipated by then to do so. Then I thought of the great American writer Thomas Wolfe, whose editor told him to write about heroes in search of father figures.

*I* think that most Canadian and American novels, if they are to be true to life, should feature heroes and heroines in search of *mother* figures. A mother is always much more valuable than a father.

I don't want another father. Neither does Willard Salmon or Centrick Cline.

?

Just as Centrick Cline was bitching at Billy Pope in the used-trucks section of the dealership, a man guilty of matricide was flying a private plane at Abbotsford International Airport, not far from the Ford truck dealership. This man, Walter Bliss, was Willard Salmon's patron. He killed his mother, not deliberately, while they were sailing about in the Burrard Inlet. She was Women's Contract Bridge Champion of Canada the year before Lovejoy killed her.

?

The two physicians on board the *Veronica* as it sped towards the disaster: Jaz Johal, from India, and Rupinder Bhutto from Pakistan, two countries known for being unable to feed their people sometimes. Willard Salmon wrote about both places in his book *What the Man Doesn't Want You to Know*. Centrick Cline read in that book that free will was a very special and dangerous thing to have, and that the one person who has such a thing should consider it more a curse than a blessing.

?

Here was why Vancouver, and the rest of Canada, had so many foreign-born doctors: Canada did not produce nearly enough doctors through its own medical schools, so it had to go hire those from other countries, and the Third World doctors worked for the least money.

?

Centrick Cline was hustled aboard the *Veronica*. So was Willard Salmon, but Willard was mostly uninjured and seated himself without assistance. He had manhandled Centrick Cline when Centrick dragged Agnes Semko out into the parking lot to manhandle her because his mental illness told him she had it coming.

Centrick had already broken her nose and knocked out two teeth in his office. He dragged her outside and presented to the medium-large crowd that had spilled out from the cocktail lounge of the Best Western. "Best piece of ass in British Columbia," he told the crowd. "Pull off her panties and let her ride your dick, and she'll say 'I love you' but she won't shut up till you buy her a Tim Hortons franchise."

That's what he said. Then Salmon grabbed him from behind.

Salmon's meant to put his hand other Centrick's mouth but his finger ended up in Centrick's mouth and Centrick bit off Salmon's fingernail and all the finger attached to it. Centrick then let go of Agnes, and she crumpled to the ground, her hands covering her nose. Then she lost consciousness and her hands fell away. Everyone saw all the blood on her face. Centrick took Salmon's fingertip out of his mouth, waved it around, put it back into his mouth and swallowed. Then he smiled.

?

Willard Salmon chose not to lie down in the *Veronica*. He sat down in a deep leather seat right behind Keegan Edwards, the driver. When Keegan asked him what his problem was, Salmon showed him his partly mutilated hand, which he had covered with a handkerchief.

"I don't get mad, I get even!" yelled Centrick from the rear of the *Veronica*.

?

"Keep your friends close but your enemies closer!" yelled Centric. Most of what he had done in the past hour or so had been bad and wrong, but at least he hadn't killed Billy Pope, who was back among the used trucks. Unharmed, he was picking up a neckchain that I had tossed out there so he could find it.

Myself, I stood back and watched the violence, even though I had created Centrick and his violence and his mental illness. You can do that when you write these stories and create these characters. *Their* problems are not *yours*.

?

This is not the kind of novel in which the bad guys are punished and the bad guys are rewarded. Centrick harmed only one person who deserved to be punished: Mike Fillo, the service technician who raped Ronaye Bardell in the parking lot of the Pacific Coliseum during the Pacific National Exhibition.

?

Mike Fillo was repairing an appliance in the kitchen of the Best Western when Centrick Cline went on his rampage.

He had stepped outside to get some fresh air and was thinking about smoking a Players cigarette when Centrick rushed up to him. Centrick had just swallowed the fingertip of Willard Salmon. Mike and Centrick knew each other reasonably well because Centrick had once sold Mike a Ford F150 truck. Mike claimed it was a lemon. A lemon was a malfunctioning vehicle that no one could seem to repair.

Centrick had his mechanics try several times to fix the vehicle—all at his expense—in an attempt to regain Fillo's goodwill. But Fillo finally spray-painted THIS TRUCK IS A PIECE OF SHIT on the truck as he drove it around town.

The *real* problem with the truck was that one of Fillo's neighbors was a kid who, as a practical joke, poured milk into the truck's gas tank.

Well, when Centrick extended his right hand to Fillo, Fillo grabbed the hand and shook it. In their culture, handshakes were a greeting exchanged between two people. Many people believed that much information could be exchanged by two men as they shook hands. A weak, flaccid handshake meant that at least one of the men was dishonest or homosexual. Centrick Cline and Fillo gave each other a firm, masculine handshake, to prove to themselves and each other that they were not homosexuals.

So Centrick held onto Mike as if all were well between the two men, and with his free hand he made a sort of cup which he bashed against Mike's ear, causing Mike excruciating pain and causing him to lose eight-five percent of his hearing in that ear for the rest of his life.

?

So Mike was in the ambulance, too—he sat up like Willard Salmon. Agnes Semko lay done, out cold but whimpering. Kiesha Beeman sat up but probably should have been flat on her back. Her jaw had been fractured. Blondie Cline, his face a pulpy mess. Jaz Johal had shot him up with morphine.

There were five other victims. Three of them were white people from New Brunswick who were in Vancouver only because they were on their way to Victoria, which was on Vancouver Island. Vancouver as a city did not interest them very much; they were just passing through. They didn't pass through fast enough; Centrick Cline assaulted them in the parking lot of the Best Western.

# EPILOGUE

The hospital's emergency room was vast. After Willard Salmon had the stump of his finger disinfected, trimmed and bandaged, they told him to go to the cashier's office. He needed to fill out certain forms because he had not filled out his tax returns in years and therefore was not a client of the Medical Services Plan of British Columbia. He had no money, no bank account, *nada*.

On his way to the cashier's office he got lost, as many others had. He easily found his way into the morgue by accident, as many others had. He started pondering his own mortality, as many others had when being around dead people at funerals or in cemeteries.

Salmon kept walking. By and by he found stairs, so he climbed them and presently walked past rooms where people were recovering from a variety of conditions. He passed a room, a very expensive private one. Its door was wide open and he looked inside to see a young black man. His bedside telephone was white; he also had a color TV and boxes of chocolates and bouquets of flowers. His name was Quintin Moore, and he was a pimp who operated out of one of the city's most popular highrise hotels. At only twenty-five years old, he had already become a millionaire many times over.

Visiting hours had ended, so all of his "bitches" had left, but their pungent perfume lingered in the air. Salmon blinked and his eyes began to tear up from the perfume suspended in the air. Quintin Moore had just snorted some cocaine, so his perceptions were much keener than they usually were. At such times he was deeply thrilled to be a young man with lots of money; he wished he could simply go through life high on cocaine, but he knew that was not possible so he enjoyed the cocaine experience as much as he could while it lasted.

While high on cocaine, Quintin Moore smiled at Willard Salmon and said, "Hey man, what up?" He had had his foot amputated earlier that day by Wang

Kang, but it did not matter to him at that moment. It would matter later on, but not as he spoke to Salmon. "What up man?" he asked, smiling. He wanted nothing from Willard Salmon; it was the cocaine talking. Cocaine made Quintin even friendlier than usual, and usually he was a very friendly man. Elgin laughed. His laugh was low and soft and deep. His smile was big and white.

Salmon came over and stood at the foot of Quintin's bed. Salmon had no empathy or compassion for the black man; he was merely being a human machine, and human machines often, when they heard someone say, "Hey man, what up?" came a little bit closer to the other human machine who asked the question.

Quintin Moore lured people in all the time. That was how he had become a pimp; with little effort he gave young women the impression that he was God's representative on Earth and they needed to work for him if they wanted to get to heaven. Everett manipulated and exploited people because it was in his nature to do so, but in Salmon's case he decided he had nothing to gain from Salmon. All he said was,

"I think I'm dying."

"Then call the nurse," replied Salmon.

Quintin shook his head. "My dying is gradual."

"Is that good or bad?"

Quintin ignored this. "I need you to do me a favor."

"What favor?"

Quintin had no favor in mind, but he soon thought of one. Among his greatest pleasures in life was getting favors from others. "Listen as I whistle." So he whistled as Salmon listened.

?

The University of British Columbia Festival of the Literary Arts was postponed due to insanity. Barry Doyle, the chairman, arrived at the hospital in his limousine, dressed like a black guy, to offer his condolences to Kiesha Beeman and Willard Salmon. Salmon wasn't there. Kiesha Beeman had fallen asleep from the morphine they had given her.

Willard Salmon assumed that the Literary Arts Festival would still happen that evening. He had no money to get a bus or taxi, so he walked to the venue. He walked and walked till he reached a point of light that he knew was the University of British Columbia Center for the Literary Arts. As he got closer to that point of light it got bigger. Once he got there he would feel better because there would be food inside.

?

I sat waiting for him near the University of British Columbia. I was in a Nissan Sentra I had rented from Enterprise with my American Express card. I got out of the car because my legs had cramped up and I needed to stretch them. I was out near the University of British Columbia, which over the years had become affordable to nobody who was a student at the U. Those students whose families had lots of money attended American or European universities.

?

That part of town was quiet, although maybe it shouldn't have been. Universities should be places where young people stayed up late and studied or drank beer.

When I got out of the car I was almost attacked by a dog, a big one like a German shepherd or something.

?

Check this out: The dog's name was *Tuffy*. He patrolled the area at night because the land and property were so valuable. His trainers had taught him that his job was to attack, kill and eat. The dog had no conscience about any of it; he just did his job. The only thing stopping him from mauling me was the fence between us. He barked and snarled and jumped at me but slammed against the fence instead.

?

As always, I looked into the distance and thought of the Beeman mansion, which was where Kiesha Beeman had grown up. To grow up in a mansion near the University of British Columbia was a pretty terrific thing, I thought. But the Beemans were artistic, creative people, not astute businesspeople, and at some point they mismanaged their money and had to sell their mansion. The buyers were Barry Doyle's parents and they kept it for a time. Now Barry Doyle wanted, or at least was willing, to donate his mansion to the U. so long as the U. agreed to convert it into student housing and rename it for Kimberly Doyle.

?

I stood there and stared at the Beeman mansion, not thinking that Tuffy may get over the fence and rip out my jugular. Willard Salmon came closer to me. I felt almost unconcerned about him, even though the two of us had many remarkable things to say to each other about my having created him.

I thought instead of my maternal grandfather, who had been one of the most prominent architects in British Columbia. He had designed some wonderful houses for Canuck millionaires. Those homes were now mortuaries, business schools, parking lots and other things. My mum drove me around Vancouver once, pointing out houses and factories my grandfather had designed.

Willard Salmon was near me now and coming closer. I freaked him out. I looked at him and he looked at me. The silent message I had for him was, "I have some good news for you."

Then Tuffy attacked.

?

I saw the beast out of my peripheral vision. He was the most menacing creature I had ever beheld.

My eyes said to my brain, "Uh oh."

I ran like hell and leaped over a parked car. Salmon watched me from a distance, unsure of who I was and who Tuffy was and why I had jumped over that car.

Salom had already had a long and difficult day. Too bad for him.

?

I ended up in the middle of University Avenue.

Tuffy couldn't get over the fence. Gravity slammed him back down onto the concrete. Willard Salmon turned away and started hurrying towards the U. I yelled his name but that made him walk faster.

I jumped into my car and chased him. He was walking mighty fast for a man his age.

I rolled down my window and yelled, "Mr. Salmon! Mr. Salmon! I want to talk to you!"

Being called by name got his attention. He turned around and faced me.

"I'm your friend!" I yelled. "I have some good things to tell you!"

"Are you from the Literary Arts Festival?"

"I am your creator. I am a novelist and I created you for use in this novel."

"That right, eh?"

"Yes. We're near the of this novel. Do you have any questions you would like to ask me?"

"Can't think of anything just yet."

"Well, you may be interested in knowing that you're going to win the Nobel Prize for Medicine in the years ahead."

"Yeah, right."

"It's true. I've also arranged for you to contract with a prestigious publisher. No more smut books for you."

"How nice for me."

"If I were you, I would be asking many questions."

"Are you packed?" he asked.

"What?"

"You know—do you have a gun?"

I laughed. "I don't need a gun, Mr. Salmon. I just write things down and you become whatever I want you to be."

?

"I think you're a fuckin' lunatic," he said.

"Check this out." I transported him to New York City, then Paris, then Sao Paulo, then back to Vancouver. "See what I can do?" He looked the way my mum and Blondie Cline's mum looked whenever they got freaked out.

?

I got out of my rental car and said, "Mr. Salmon, I love you. I have broken you into a zillion pieces, but I want to make you whole again. I want you to see what I have in my hand."

My hand was empty, but since I was his creator, he would see whatever I wished.

"Willard," I said, "what do I have in my hand?"

"An apple." He looked as old and haggard as my mum looked before she died. My dad had died years earlier and my mum's health had been destroyed by age and disease.

?

"I am pushing fifty, Mr. Salmon," I told him. "I'm preparing myself for whatever time I have left. Part of my preparation is to set free all of the characters who have populated my novels. Go! Be free!"

Actually, *I* disappeared.